# THE
# BLUE
# DARTER

# THE BLUE DARTER

## AND OTHER SPORTS STORIES
### Compiled by the Editors
### of
### Highlights for Children

# CONTENTS

# The Blue Darter

By Judith Logan Lehne

I stood in a corner of the dugout, making circles in the dirt with my shoe, just listening.

"We *gave* them the game," Lyle said. His hair and his "Team Captain" shirt were soaked with sweat. "We played terrible."

Paul nodded and pointed his finger at Julio. "You call yourself a pitcher? You practically threw the ball right at their bats!"

"Everybody has a bad day," I said to Lyle. "Why didn't you put Lindsay in? Her Blue Darter pitch was just what we needed today." Lindsay looked over at me, and her eyes seemed to say thanks.

"Get real, Jonathan," Lyle said, moving a huge wad of gum inside his cheek. "It's bad enough I let you talk us into having a girl on the team. The Orioles would've laughed us off the field if we had let her pitch."

Lindsay pulled off her cap and shook out her long ponytail. "The score was 18 to 6, Lyle!" she said. "The Orioles got their laughs anyway."

"Well, the Cubs won't be laughing tomorrow," Lyle said. He grabbed his mitt. "Let's practice!"

Everyone tromped to the field.

"Jonathan," Paul said, "you're our best hitter. Tell us your secret."

"Natural talent," I said, shrugging. I felt Lindsay's eyes on me. I knew what she wanted me to tell them. I owed my batting success to her—and the hours of practice with her grandfather. He's the one who taught her the Blue Darter. I never got the hang of it, but Lindsay could whistle the ball off her fingers and make it curve crazily when I was in mid-swing. It was because of Lindsay's Blue Darter that I was a good batter. But I couldn't tell the guys that. I just couldn't.

Walking home, Lindsay was silent. When we reached her house, she turned and glared.

"You could have told them, Jonathan," she said between clenched teeth. "Maybe they'd have let me pitch tomorrow."

I glared back. "You want me to make a fool of myself? When you're not around, they always tease me. If they knew you helped my batting . . . "

She looked as though she might cry, but I kept yelling. "I got you on the team. Isn't that enough?"

"This isn't about *baseball*," she said. Her ponytail whipped across her face as she stomped away.

All night I kept hearing Lindsay saying, "This isn't about baseball." What did she mean?

Before the game with the Cubs, I apologized to her. "It's OK," she said. "I guess it's not easy having a girl for a best friend."

Listening to Lyle, the guys squirmed on the bench. Lindsay leaned against the dugout wall.

"Show 'em our best! No errors," Lyle said, blowing bubbles between words. "Julio, you pitch."

I looked at Lindsay, but I kept quiet.

We were first at bat. The Cubs' pitcher was good, but not great. When I stepped to the plate, Lyle was on third and Paul was on first. I looked at the dugout. Lindsay shouted, "Whack it!" My hands felt clammy.

"Strike one!" the umpire shouted. I hadn't even swung at it.

9

"Concentrate," I said to myself. The ball came toward the plate, and I swung. *Crack!* I raced to first . . . second . . . third . . . home!

After the back-slapping cheers, the game took a downward turn. The Cubs' not-so-great pitcher got better, and our hitting got worse. Julio was still in a pitching slump. By the fifth inning, we were down by seven runs.

As we took the field, I grabbed Lyle's arm. "Give Lindsay a chance," I said. The team stopped to listen. Lindsay stayed in the dugout, watching.

"No girl pitchers," Lyle snarled. "Especially not your *girlfriend*."

"She's not my . . . ," I began. I looked at Lindsay. This isn't about baseball, she'd said.

"She is my girl *friend*," I said. Someone snickered. "She's a girl, and she's my friend." I put my face close to Lyle's. "And when you see her Blue Darter pitch, you will know she's this *team's* friend, too."

"Let her pitch," Julio said.

Talking all at once, the guys nudged Lyle. "Let's see her Blue Darter!"

Lyle called Lindsay from the dugout. "You'd better be good," he said.

Lindsay stepped to the mound. "Come on, Lindsay," I cheered. "Show 'em your stuff."

She kicked dirt around, looking shy and not at all like a pitcher. The guys exchanged glances. Just wait, I wanted to tell them. They didn't have to wait long. She bent forward, threw her arm back, and whipped the ball off her fingers. It flew like an arrow until it was nearly over the plate, then it veered to the left.

"Strike one!" the umpire called.

Lindsay grinned at me and continued to hurl the Blue Darter at lightning speed, just as her grandfather had taught her. The Cubs never even scored another run.

We lost, but the Cubs weren't laughing.

Lyle came into the dugout and shook Lindsay's hand. He swallowed hard. "You're a terrific pitcher," he said. He turned to me. "And you've got a great best friend."

"I know," I said, looking at Lindsay. "True blue."

# All-Star Team

By Fern Simms

Don watched Lee dribble the ball down the court. As Don eluded a guard and slipped closer to the basket, he and Lee made eye contact. Don reached to catch the ball.

"Throw, Lee," he breathed. He knew he could make the shot. Lee's guard was right next to Lee. But in a flash, Lee shot. Don frowned. Why hadn't he tossed him the ball? The ball wobbled on the ring. Don held his breath. Then the ball leaned inward and went through the basket. He sighed heavily. It was close, but Lee had made it. Two more points for them. The score was tied.

Someone yelled, "Time out," and they grouped together, breathing heavily.

"Just two more points," said Lee, "and we'll win. Just feed me the ball, guys. I'll do the rest."

"You're greedy," said Bob Smith.

"But I make them, every time," said Lee.

"Guess you do," conceded Bob. "You're way ahead of us in total shots. But never mind that now. Let's get back out there and give it to them. And watch your fouls, guys. Come on!"

Don took his place. He watched Lee trot on the court—all confidence. He couldn't complain, but it was risky. Don's position at the time was more sure. No wonder Lee made so many baskets. He hogged the ball. The boy guarding Don nodded toward Lee. "That one of your all-stars?"

Donald shrugged. "We don't know yet. We haven't chosen the players on our team who will be in the all-star game."

The whistle blew and Bob got the ball. He tossed it to Don. Don swung away from his guard and made an underhand throw to Lee. He inched his way toward their basket, one eye on the ball. Bob had it now and passed it to Don. It was a long shot to the basket, but clear. Don had quickly side-stepped his guard. There was a chance he could make a basket.

"Don! Here!" It was Lee, nearer to the basket, and free from his guard, too. For a split second, Don was disappointed. He wanted to try that throw, but there was more of a chance if Lee made the shot. He was closer. "Good-bye, all-star team," he muttered to himself and sailed the ball straight into Lee's hands. Lee leaped and threw. The ball hit the backboard and dropped right down through the basket. The crowd roared. The game was over.

Don wondered if he would have made the basket. It would have been a grandstand play. It would have made him look good.

They sang and joked in the showers. While they dressed, Coach Adamson handed each of them a card with the list of names of all the players on their team.

"This year we are giving you the chance to pick your own stars for the special game," said the coach. "Check two players on the list, because we are allowed two men."

Don checked Bob's name. There was no doubt Bob was a good player. He hesitated at Lee's name. He was so annoyed at him that he was tempted to skip it. Then he sighed and put a check next to it. Lee was a good shot—no denying that.

The coach collected the cards. "If there are any ties, I'll make the deciding vote for the one I think is the better man. OK?"

There was a murmur of approval.

"I'll tally them up now and call out the results," said Coach Adamson.

They grouped around. Everyone's hopes were high. It was an honor to be on the all-stars. The coach looked up.

"Well, Bob is one," said the coach. "No doubt about that. But Don and Lee tied."

Don's heart leaped. He hadn't expected to come close, and here he was, tied with Lee. Lee looked over at Don and grinned. "OK, Coach, you pick. You're the one who would really know who deserves it." But Lee didn't seem worried.

"Well," said Coach Adamson, "I wish it could be both, but since it can't, I'll pick Don."

There was a loud murmur. Then Bob clapped Don on the back and said, "Congratulations!"

Don's thoughts were in such a whirl that he was the last one to gather his things in the locker room. Coach Adamson walked over to him.

Don grinned. "Hope you know what you're doing, Coach."

The coach looked directly in Don's eyes. "Believe me, I know."

Don squirmed. "Well, it's just that Lee's such a good shot. He makes most of the baskets."

"Why shouldn't he?" said Coach Adamson. "He shoots whether there's a man in a better position or not. Look, Don, you play for the team, not for yourself. That means more than being a good shot. Play the all-star game as you always play. Don't worry. I know a good man when I see one."

Don walked out of the room with his head high. He felt like giving a couple of whoops. Then he saw Lee waiting for him. He stopped.

"Hi, Lee." Suddenly he felt sorry for Lee. "I guess you don't care, but I'd like you to know I picked you for the all-stars."

Lee grinned. "That figures. And you know what? I picked you."

Don's surprise was genuine. "You did?"

"Yeah. You always give a hundred percent, and you're a team player. It paid off. Congratulations!"

# Backstroke!

By Laura Potter

Amy traced the engraved letters of the trophy with her finger. "Backstroke . . . Third Place . . . Amy Jenkins," she murmured. Her lips trembled, and a salty tear trickled down her cheek. "I should have swum freestyle. I could have *won* that race," she thought, placing the trophy on the empty shelf in her new bedroom in the unfamiliar New York City apartment.

Her mind wandered back home to Cape Cod and to the advice her swimming coach had offered just before that last, frustrating meet. "You should get good at more than one stroke," he had told her. "Don't always enter the freestyle." And so Amy had entered the backstroke event, swimming from the dock to a raft anchored one hundred yards away. But she kept going off course and had to stop to get her bearings. Two faster swimmers beat her.

"What a rotten day that was," Amy grumbled as she absentmindedly resumed unpacking. "And now there won't be any more swim teams, races, or blue ribbons." Picking up a framed photograph, Amy stared at the picture of herself standing on the Falmouth town dock. Moored to a cleat, her twelve-foot skiff, the *Sand Witch,* floated alongside her.

Amy squeezed her dark eyes tight and could almost taste the ocean spray misting her face as she rode the waves in the Cape Cod coves. How she longed to wake to the impatient cries of hungry gulls, to smell the familiar oily scent of low tide, and to crunch barefoot along the shore. Amy's bare toes wriggled against the cold wooden floor, and she frowned.

Falmouth was far away now, and Manhattan seemed so unfriendly. Amy sighed. She doubted that this place would ever feel like home.

Amy turned to see her father enter with the Sunday papers under his arm. "I picked up this flyer in the lobby," he said as he handed her a printed announcement.

> **ATTENTION**
> **BOYS AND GIRLS, Ages 8 - 14**
> **COME ONE, COME ALL!**
> **LABOR DAY SWIM MEET**
> **at the Rooftop Pool**
> **PRIZES GALORE**
> **Monday, 1:00 P.M.**

"That's tomorrow," said Amy, beaming. "I think I'd better practice."

She grabbed her red, white, and blue tank suit and changed into it. "I'll be back for lunch, Mom," she called as she trotted out the front door.

Amy rode the elevator twelve flights to the rooftop pool. It was still early, and only one other swimmer had arrived. Draping her terrycloth robe over a chair, she took a deep breath, dived in, and frog-kicked underwater the length of the seventy-five-foot pool.

As her head surfaced at the far end, Amy yelped with disgust. "Chlorine!" she gasped. "This sure doesn't taste like the Atlantic Ocean." She treaded water for a moment and tried to rub her eyes.

"How can I win the race when it hurts to open my eyes underwater?" she wondered. Then suddenly her lips parted in a wide grin. "Backstroke!" She laughed. "If I swim on my back, my face won't get wet—except on the turns."

The pool was divided into five lanes. Amy knew that it would be easy to keep on course by glancing at the ropes as she swam. Her only problem would be timing her flip turns.

Amy looked around for guideposts. A ladder hung from the wall of the pool several feet from the deep end. Beside the shallow end stood a round redwood table with an orange-and-yellow beach umbrella sticking up through the center. Amy swam several practice laps using the beach umbrella and the ladder to signal the turning points. They worked out fine. Amy practiced until she felt ready for the race.

The Labor Day sun beat down on the spectators. Amy was grateful for the cool water as she waited in the pool for her race to begin. Her eyes scanned the crowd for a glimpse of her parents. Her dad raised two fingers in a V-for-Victory sign, and her mom blew her a kiss and waved. Amy flashed them a confident smile, but underwater she crossed her fingers—just for good measure.

"Swimmers, . . . mark," the official announced.

Amy took the first lane and nodded to the four strangers who were competing in the same event. "Here goes," she murmured, crouching up against the side in the shallow water.

"Get set!" The starting pistol crackled. Amy was off and stroking furiously, counting strokes as she neared the ladder marker. "Tumble back, twist, feet on the side, thrust off, break the surface," she coached herself and stroked hard to the opposite end. "Umbrella marker, flip, swoosh, kick, paddle—two more lengths to go."

At the finish line, Amy's fingers touched the wall nearly half a length ahead of the other swimmers. "Congratulations, Miss Jenkins," the official said when he handed her a blue ribbon. "I'll be coaching the swim team at the Y this October. How would you like to try out?"

"I'll be there," Amy responded happily. "Imagine, swimming all year round." She smiled. Maybe living in the city wouldn't be so bad after all.

# Carl Takes a Spill

By Mildred Bair Lissfelt

Carl and his family lived in Switzerland. One winter holiday he and two of his classmates, Will and Kurt, went with his parents and sister Marie to Zermatt to ski. There, rising above the village and its ski slopes, was the Matterhorn. Everyone was delighted to see the towering mountain again, and Marie made sketches of it in her notebook.

On their first morning the family and friends skied on the lower slopes near the village. In the afternoon the boys decided they would try the upper slopes. Marie begged to go along, and Carl reluctantly consented. They went up the mountainside by cable car and toward evening were ready to take the last run of the day.

Will and Kurt had started down, and Carl was waiting for Marie. She stood at the opposite side of the wide ski trail, looking up at the peak.

"Are you coming?" Carl asked impatiently, anxious to follow the others and get back to the inn for dinner.

"In a minute," Marie answered.

She bent to fumble with a ski strap she had already fastened, and Carl's impatience gave way to anger. Though younger than he, Marie skied almost as well. But what a dawdler! At this rate they'd be the very last to reach the village. He looked down the slope and saw his friends and other skiers zigzagging on the trail far below.

"Stay, then, as long as you like," he shouted. "I'm going."

"Wait. I'm coming."

Furious with her, Carl thrust his ski poles into the hard-packed snow and shoved off. At her cry he increased his speed. Why did she always have to be last? He'd get so far ahead of her this time that she'd never catch up.

Faster and faster he went, so absorbed in angry thoughts that he paid no attention to the warning signal—a row of orange pennants along the trail—until he had almost reached them. Too late to reduce his speed for the dangerous curve ahead, he tried to cling to the outer edge, then hit an icy spot and tumbled down the snowy bank beside it.

Sprawled on his back, with feet up and head not far from the fall line—at this place a sheer drop of many feet—Carl wondered what to do. In most spills a skier in his position could have somersaulted downward, landed on his skis, and made his way sideways up the slope. Here this was impossible because of the drop.

From where he lay he could not see the trail above the curve. But if Marie had followed, she must be close by. In an effort to stop her before she skied past him, he began calling her name.

"Marie!" he shouted over and over.

In what seemed hours but was only minutes, Marie skied around the bend and braked to a stop above him. Her cheeks were as red as her bright jacket, and the wind was whipping her hair from under her cap.

"Carl," she asked anxiously, "are you hurt?"

"Only my pride," he said. "Go on down the mountain and send help. I don't dare try to move or get up by myself."

"But that would take too long. You might freeze to death. There must be something I can do."

"Do as I say," Carl ordered. He was no longer angry except with himself. And he could not let Marie risk herself for him. "Go on down. Tell the Ski Patrol."

"I won't go without you," Marie said. "If we don't get back soon, they'll come looking for us."

She started down the slope toward him, stepping sideways as they had been taught in ski class. Carl watched her anxiously. One false move and she could easily slide over the cliff. She came down cautiously until she reached him.

"Should I take off your skis?" she asked.

"Yes, please. Be sure to stick the ends deep into the snow," he added, "so they won't slide away."

She took off one ski and plunged it into the snow above her. She did the same with the other.

"What now?" she asked.

"You know so much," he mocked, "what do you suggest?" But this was no time for joking, and he raised one of the ski poles attached to his wrist and held the free end toward her. "Take hold," he said. "Don't pull. Just dig in farther with your skis, lean back, and brace yourself while I hold on."

When she had followed his instructions, Carl dug into the snow with his other pole. Supporting himself with both poles, he pulled himself up. Before his shoes could sink too deeply, he started climbing, shifting his ski poles as he went. Marie followed slowly. Both of them sighed with relief when they reached the trail.

"I've got to get these skis on," Carl said, "without one of them slipping away."

"I'll stand below you and catch it if it gets away," Marie said.

As soon as he was ready, he told her to go ahead and set the speed. "She's a good skier," he thought as she shoved off.

He followed, zigzagging down the trail, through the woods, and on to the edge of the village. There Carl's friends were waiting, wondering what had happened. When Carl told them, Kurt slapped him on the back.

"So the best skier took a spill," he joked.

"That's right," Carl replied good-naturedly. He smiled at Marie and added, "Every skier takes a spill once in a while. But not everyone has a little sister on hand to come to the rescue."

# The Softball Switcharound

By Helen Kronberg

Katie kicked a dandelion. "Sandy *would* get to pitch," she said.

Sue rolled her bike away from the rack. "You have to admit she's pretty good."

Katie snorted and angrily pedaled away. "It sure doesn't hurt to have her aunt as the coach."

"You're just jealous." Sue peered at Katie. "You *are* jealous, aren't you? You wanted to be the pitcher this year."

"So what?" Katie asked.

"But you're a good outfielder."

Katie shrugged and looked down.

"And you're one of the best batters on the team," Sue added.

"Everybody gets to bat," Katie said. "But the game depends on the pitcher. That's Sandy."

Sue's mother waved from the porch. "See you," Sue said.

"See you," Katie repeated. She pedaled up the drive next door and slid to a stop. She barged through the kitchen door, grabbed an apple from a bowl on the table, and went to her room. Katie liked Coach Kelly, but she'd like her better if she weren't Sandy's aunt.

"Wow, you sure are grumpy," her brother said.

Katie ignored him.

At the next practice Coach Kelly called the players together. "We're going to do some shifting around. I have the feeling that some of you are not too happy with your positions. We want a good team, but most of all we want to have fun. Softball should be fun."

Sue poked Katie. "Hey, maybe you'll get a chance to pitch after all."

Practice lasted a long time. Everyone who wanted to pitch was given a chance.

After practice Katie hopped on her bike and spun around. "I did OK on the mound."

"You do a lot better as an outfielder," Sue said.

Katie tossed her hair. "I just need practice. Do you think the coach will let me pitch in the game this weekend?"

"Maybe," Sue said.

Katie twirled her glove into the air and caught it with one hand. "I can see it now: 'The Hawks win another shutout. The pitcher? Katie Doyle, the winningest pitcher around.'"

"Well, you never know," Sue said. "Good luck."

Katie practiced her pitching. Sometimes Sue helped. Sometimes Katie pitched to her dad or her brother. But every day was practice day.

Finally she asked Coach Kelly to let her pitch in a game.

"Are you sure you want to?" Coach asked. "You're such a good outfielder."

"Please?" Katie asked. "I've practiced a lot."

Coach Kelly smiled. "OK, Katie. We'll miss you in the outfield. But we'll let you and Sandy take turns for one game. How's that?"

"Terrific," Katie shouted.

The day of the game against the Jets arrived. Katie bubbled with excitement.

Sandy took the mound first. She pitched for two innings with no score on either side. Then it was Katie's turn.

She walked to the mound feeling eight feet tall. She cradled the ball in her hand, got just the right grip, and threw, feeling a surge of joy as the ball left her hand.

*Crack!*

Katie's mouth fell open. Her heart sank clear to her toes. The ball sailed high over her head. "You've got it, Sandy," she yelled. But Sandy didn't have it. The ball slipped right through Sandy's grasp. The Jets' batter raced around the bases and scored.

There were other hits, but no more runs. Katie left the mound with a sigh of relief.

The Hawks managed to score twice. They were ahead. But Katie was nervous about taking the mound again. "Sandy can pitch," she said.

Coach Kelly shook her head. "It's still your turn. If you like, Sandy will pitch the last two innings."

Katie gulped and nodded. As she walked to the mound, she thought about the Jets' lineup. She sized up each batter. Then she did her best. She held her breath every time the ball was hit, but the Jets managed only a few short pop-ups.

The Hawks did no better. By the final inning they were still only one run ahead. Sandy was back on the mound. Katie was in the outfield. There were two outs and a runner on second.

*Crack!* "It's a home run!" somebody shouted.

But they shouted too soon. Katie raced backward and was under it with sure hands. The game was over.

Katie ran to the infield and grinned at Sandy. "You're a good pitcher, but you need practice catching those long fly balls."

Sandy nodded. "I felt awful. It was my fault when they scored."

Katie shook her head. "It was my fault. I thought pitching would make me a star. I wasn't thinking about what was best for the team." She laughed. "Besides, like Coach says, softball should be fun."

The girls locked arms and joined their teammates in celebration.

# The Bulldozers

By Marilyn Bissell

Luis finished his lunch in a hurry, then went to get his baseball glove and ball from the bedroom closet. He ran out the door and took two stairs at a time all the way down the three flights to the door at the front of the apartment building.

It was a beautiful Saturday—sunny and warm. He could feel the heat bounce back at him from the pavement.

Luis lived on a busy street lined with apartment buildings just like the one where he lived. There were eight families in each building, so there were always plenty of other kids around. Some of his friends were already outside.

"Hey, Luis! Want to play catch?" yelled Pete from the third building away.

"Where?" hollered Luis.

"Right here. Where else could we play?"

Where else indeed? His mother wouldn't let him play in the street. And he didn't have a bike to ride to the school yard as the high school boys did. The only place to play was right here on the sidewalk between the buildings and the street. A guy could hardly improve his pitching or try to bat in such a small space.

Luis and Pete tossed the ball back and forth for a while and then went to Tony's store for a can of soda. The only thing between Pete's building and Tony's store was a messy vacant lot.

As the boys walked past the empty lot, they picked a few wild flowers that grew among the weeds. Luis's mother called the lot a "jungle" and had complained to the city about it. But she had been told that the lot belonged to Tony, and it was up to him to clean it up.

At Tony's, Luis chose orange soda; Pete had a root beer. They sat at the counter while they drank their sodas.

"Hey, Tony. What are you going to do with that lot next door?" asked Luis.

Tony was slicing cold cuts for a customer. "What do you mean?" he asked.

"I mean, are you going to build there?"

"Ha! Build? Do I look like a millionaire?"

"Well, aren't you going to clean it up and use it for something?"

"No! Who's got time for that?"

When Luis and Pete finished their drinks, they hopped off their chairs and went out again.

"Oh, no!" said Pete. "Look."

A group of girls had marked hopscotch squares on the sidewalk and were playing right in the space the boys needed to play catch!

As they were passing the lot again, Luis stopped suddenly. He looked at the mess.

"Do you think we could do it?" he asked.

"Do what?" asked Pete.

"Clean up this lot ourselves."

"Are you kidding? My mother says there are mice and thorns and broken glass there!"

"The mice are only there because the weeds give them a hiding place. If we clean out the weeds, the mice will go away."

"But it belongs to Tony," said Pete.

"Tony isn't using it. He said so himself."

"Let's ask!" said Pete.

They ran back to the store and found Tony putting bags of potato chips on a rack.

"Tony! Tony! If we clean up your lot, could we use it for a playground?" gasped Luis.

"Clean it up? By yourselves? It would take you kids a year."

"Not if the other kids on the block help, too," urged Luis. "We really need room to practice baseball, Tony."

"Oh, please," begged Pete, dropping to his knees with his hands folded.

Tony laughed at the boys. "OK, you two. Go ahead and try. But I think you need a bulldozer."

As the days passed, the boys agreed that it was a huge job. They had gone from building to building asking all the kids who were old enough to help. Many agreed. Some parents wouldn't let their children help, fearing that they might get hurt on broken glass or rusty metal.

Tony helped a lot, too. He gave the children empty cartons to fill with the weeds they pulled. He even dug out some thorny plants himself when there were no customers in his store.

Slowly but surely the crowd of children cleared the "jungle." Parents began to watch and help after they came home from work.

Finally, the whole lot was bare, and Luis and Pete thought the red clay was the prettiest sight they'd ever seen.

The kids in the neighborhood organized ball teams. Luis's team came from the even-numbered apartments. Pete's team was from those with odd numbers. Luis called them the "Odd Balls," and Pete laughed.

Everyone on the block agreed that Tony should be thanked for letting them use his lot, so Luis's mother asked each member of his team to bring her a plain T-shirt. At the very first game to be played on their new field, Tony was amazed to see the name Luis's mother had put on the back of each boy's shirt—*Tony's Bulldozers*.

Tony never missed a game all season. He was there to cheer on his *Bulldozers*. The only time he left was between innings, when his store filled with more customers than he had ever had before.

# SHAD WITH DAD

By David Lubar

"Where are you going, Dad?" Alison asked, though she already knew the answer. Her father was wearing a vest and carrying his tackle box.

"Bowling," he said with a wink.

"And if you don't get all the pins, you can knock them down with that," she said, pointing to his fishing rod. "Can I come?"

"I don't know," he said. "This isn't like regular fishing. I'm going for shad, and they're a bit tricky. You have to cast way out to the middle of the river to reach them. I don't think you can cast that far yet."

"I can try." Alison gave him her best how-can-you-bear-to-go-without-me look.

"OK, fishing buddy. Get your stuff."

"Great." Alison got her rod and climbed into the car. "What are shad?" she asked on the way to the river. Alison had caught lots of different fish. She especially liked rainbow trout, because they were so pretty, and smallmouth bass, because they were so strong.

"They're actually ocean fish," Dad said. "Shad are born in the river, then they swim to the ocean. After they grow up, they return to the river to lay their eggs. They're hard to get because they stick to the deep part of the river."

"I would too, if I knew all those people were trying to catch me," Alison said as they drove up the highway along the Delaware River. The bank on the Pennsylvania side was lined with people. Looking across, she saw that there were just as many people on the New Jersey side.

"It's like this every April," Dad explained. "Shad are only around for a few months, and everyone wants a chance to catch one."

"They are sure working hard at it." Alison watched the men and women on the bank cast their lines far out toward the middle of the river. She didn't see any kids her age.

Dad was right, she realized as she got her small pole out of the car. There was no way she could cast that far, not without a rocket tied to her line. But she was out with Dad, and that was fun.

"Now don't wander off," he said as they walked toward the river. "You know the rules."

Alison nodded. Her dad had strict rules about fishing. And she had to admit that she had a habit of wandering off, though she preferred to think of it as being independent. This wasn't much of a problem in town, but it could be big trouble if she went her own way in the woods. They don't put street signs on trees.

"I'll be right here," she said.

She sat on a large, flat rock and watched the activity around her. Like most of the other people, Dad would cast far out, let the line drift while jigging the rod, then reel the line in again. Once in a while someone would shout "Fish on!" and try to land a shad. Her dad finally hooked one, too, but it leaped out of the water, shook its head, and threw off the hook.

"Getting bored?" he asked after a while.

"No, just watching everybody else," Alison said. Actually, it was fun being the only one who wasn't fishing. Sometimes she didn't want to be part of the crowd. But it sure would be exciting if she were one of the people to catch a shad.

A few more people caught shad. One woman landed a giant carp. Then everything became very quiet once again.

"The fish seem to come and go," Alison said, noticing a pattern in the action.

"They come by in schools," Dad said. "It's partly a matter of luck. But it helps to think like a fish." He made a fish face at her, puffing his cheeks and sticking out his lips.

Or like a kid, she thought. She picked up her rod and made a short cast into the river, let the line drift, then reeled it back.

Dad looked at her and smiled, but didn't say a thing. Alison smiled back, made a fish face at him, and made another cast. Then she made another, and another. For a while she counted her casts. Somewhere around thirty she lost track.

"Last cast" she kept telling herself, but each time she decided to try once more. Suddenly, the rod was almost pulled from her hands. "Dad!" she shouted as something very strong began yanking line from her reel.

"Easy," he answered. "Take your time. Don't pull too hard. You know how to do it."

She did. Alison worked the fish carefully, letting it run when it wanted and reeling in line when she could. Twice the shad jumped out of the water. People were watching, but she was too busy to notice. This fish wasn't going to break her line and get away. After a lengthy struggle she brought it close to shore, and her dad scooped it up in a net.

"It's beautiful," Alison said as Dad unhooked the fish. It was big and strong and shinier than all the coins in the world.

"I never would have believed you'd catch a shad that close to shore," Dad said, shaking his head and smiling. "They are usually out in the deep part."

"Everyone was trying hard to think like a fish," Alison said, noticing that a lot of people were listening to her. "I wondered if sometimes a fish might think like a kid. If I had to swim up this whole river, I don't think I'd follow the crowd all the time."

Alison made another short cast. She smiled as she noticed that she wasn't the only one casting close to shore.

# Reading the Signals

By Cris Peterson

The football sailed through the air in a perfect spiral. Watching the quarterback from the sideline, Rick muttered to himself, "I wish I could tie both of his shoelaces together."

Only last week a new kid had enrolled at Rick's school. Within forty-eight hours at Grantsburg Middle School it seemed that with his easy smile and joking manner, Brian had made more friends than Rick had made in a lifetime.

And now at football practice after school, Coach Johnson was trying Brian in Rick's position as the quarterback on the team.

At the end of practice, the players flocked around Brian. Rick heaved a frustrated sigh. "Why does Brian have to be on my team?" he thought. He wished Brian hadn't moved to Grantsburg.

The following morning Rick's glum mood had not brightened much as he shuffled to his desk in social studies. Brian smiled a greeting from across the aisle, but Rick ignored him.

"We'll begin reading at the top of page thirty-eight," Mrs. Greenwood said.

Books thudded. Pages rattled. Rick rolled his eyes. He hated it when Mrs. Greenwood made them read out loud.

"Brian, you may begin," she said.

Rick turned to watch. Brian's smile faded. He stared at his book in alarm.

"By . . . the . . . 1750s," he began, "th . . . the . . . Middle . . . Col . . . Col . . . Colonies . . . " As Brian scowled at the page, his ears turned pink and then beet red. Slowly, painfully, Brian limped through the paragraph.

"Rick, continue, please," said Mrs. Greenwood.

Attempting to fill the uneasy silence, Rick sped through the next three paragraphs.

That night at supper he told his family about Brian. "You should have seen his face when Mrs. Greenwood asked him to read. He turned purple!"

"Why was he so upset?" Mom asked.

"He can hardly read," Rick answered. "Maybe he's dumb. Everybody should be able to read by the fifth grade."

"I had trouble learning to read," Dad said.

Rick stared at his father. "But you're smart! You're an architect."

"Just the same, I couldn't read and I felt dumb," Dad repeated. "A good friend helped me wade through the books I had to read. After years of practice, it finally started to get easier."

Practice reading? Rick couldn't imagine having so much trouble with reading. Brian must feel miserable, he thought.

The next morning the fifth-grade team gathered at the high school field for the first Saturday scrimmage of the season. The field seemed gigantic compared with Grantsburg's playground. Rick parked his bike and joined the group of players gathered around Coach Johnson.

"Rick, you'll call the signals today," Coach said.

Rick nodded and glanced at Brian, who stared at the ground. This is my chance to show the team what I can do, Rick thought. But in the first quarter, Rick's team failed to move the ball. The other school did better, but both sides were scoreless when the whistle blew.

On the first play of the second quarter, Rick faked a hand-off, swung to the left, and broke through the line for an eight-yard gain. Finally, he felt some of his confidence returning.

On the second down, as he dropped back to pass, the ball slipped from his grasp. Scrambling, he fell on it but took a five-yard loss.

Third down and seven yards left to go, Rick thought. The sweat trickling between his shoulder blades felt like ants crawling on his back. "I have to make this one," he mumbled to himself.

"Ready, set," Rick's voice rang out. "Hut! Hut!"

He took the snap and back-pedaled, scanning the field for a receiver. As the defense closed in on him, he tossed a long wobbly pass toward the sideline. An opponent snatched the ball in midair and tore down the field toward the opposite goal. Rick gave chase, hoping to catch the ball carrier and force him out of bounds.

Too late. Touchdown.

Rick felt as if he had been tackled by the front line of the Green Bay Packers. He focused on a clump of grass at his feet, trying to catch his breath. Then he turned and trudged to the sideline.

"I just don't have it today," Rick told Coach Johnson. "Maybe Brian should take over."

The coach studied Rick's face, then nodded and called to Brian.

"We need you to quarterback," Rick blurted out before the coach could explain. "I blew it."

Brian silently listened to the coach's instructions, then ran out to join the rest of the team.

"Rick, you go in for Tim as wide receiver," Coach Johnson said. Rick raced back onto the playing field.

The kickoff was returned to the 30-yard line. The teams lined up, with Brian behind the center and Rick split wide to the right.

Brian's first pass was incomplete. The pressure got worse.

For a second time Brian drifted back, the ball at his ear. Rick sidestepped a defender and sprinted downfield. He turned just as Brian fired a bullet pass in his direction.

Leaping into the air, Rick grabbed the ball. He tucked it under his arm and streaked along the sideline. As an opponent reached out for him, Rick dived toward the end zone.

Touchdown!

Brian raced to the end zone. "What a great catch!" he shouted, helping Rick get to his feet.

Rick brushed off the dust from his jersey. Surrounded by cheering teammates, they headed for the sideline. "I wish I could pass like you do," Rick said.

"I'll help you if you want me to," Brian offered. Kicking the ground, he frowned at Rick and muttered, "I wish I could read like I pass."

Rick tossed Brian the ball and grinned. "I can help you with reading. If both of us practice, we'll be unbeatable!"

# Thin Ice

By Jack W. Hankins

Jim crouched, digging his worn, old skates into the holes he'd chipped in the ice. He glanced up the line at the other contestants on the frozen river. The official starter was standing at one end of the line, urging on those who weren't ready yet. In his hand was the little pistol he would use to signal the beginning of the race.

With a frown on his usually smiling face, Jim turned to the redheaded boy crouched beside him. "Drew," Jim said, "about that shortcut . . . "

But Drew apparently didn't hear him. He was busily tightening the laces on one of his skates. Jim glanced again at the starter. Was Drew going to take the shortcut?

Yesterday he and Drew had skated the course over which the race was to be run. Drew was new to town and had never been in the race before. He wanted to learn the racecourse, which began at the old bridge and ended at the marker on the ice upstream. They had reached the place where the river forked, one part going almost directly toward the marker, the other curving far out around an island. Jim had taken the long way.

"Why don't you go the other way?" Drew asked. "It's shorter."

Jim stopped. "I don't know," he answered. His face looked puzzled. "As long as I've been skating, the race has always been over the long way."

"Isn't the prize given to the person who makes the fastest time between the bridge and marker?"

It was. But why hadn't anyone ever gone the short way?

"Maybe the ice is bad the other way."

So Jim and Drew had investigated the shortcut. The ice over it had been far better than over the long way, unusually clear, glass smooth. Why hadn't someone gone this way in the race? Why didn't everybody? Just then some men had driven down to the edge of the river in a truck and had gotten out, and Jim and Drew had gone on.

Then Drew suggested that they secretly take the shortcut in the race. Going that way, they would be sure to win. It would be fair. The prize of brand-new skates was to go to the skater who traveled fastest between the bridge and marker. No route had been named.

But was it fair? And was Drew going to take the shortcut? If Drew took it, Jim would have to, if he were going to win the new skates to replace his old ones. Anyone who took the shortcut would be sure to win.

Jim turned to Drew, but he was still lacing his skate with frantic haste. Well, at least Jim could find out if racing over the shortcut was fair. He could ask the starter.

But just as Jim straightened to skate toward him, the starter called, "On your mark! Get set!" and raised his pistol.

Jim crouched again. What should he do?

At the crack of the pistol, Jim flashed forward with the rest. Soon he was leading. He had expected to, of course, for he had practiced much more than the others. He needed to win. His old skates were almost worn out. To make sure that they wouldn't give way during the race, he had wound them with so much wire and twine that it would take him an hour to get them off. He just had to win those new skates. But would Drew take the shortcut?

Then Jim had an idea. He would wait and see what Drew did. If Drew took the shortcut, he would; if Drew didn't, he wouldn't. That was the solution to this problem. He slowed down, waiting for Drew to catch up with him.

But Drew didn't. Jim skated slower and slower. More and more of the racers passed him. Still Drew lagged far behind. Drew was either a slow skater, or he had decided to take the shortcut and knew he didn't have to hurry.

At last Jim reached the fork in the river. Drew was still far down the ice. The others had passed him. What should he do? He couldn't wait much longer. If Drew decided not to take the shortcut, he would now have to work hard to catch up with the others and win. If . . .

Coming almost to a stop, Jim gazed back at slow-skating Drew, then at the rest of the racers far ahead. He knew he could wait no longer. He would have to go on and skate the race of his life. And just hope that Drew wouldn't take the shortcut and beat him!

Then Jim skated as hard as he could. It seemed as though he would never catch up with the others, but suddenly he was even with them and drawing ahead. He could see the marker for the finish line. Jim glanced over his shoulder back down the river. Drew wasn't coming! Drew must have taken the shortcut—and had won the race and the skates.

There was a considerable crowd at the finish line when Jim flashed across. But where was Drew? Had he already won and gone home?

Then Jim heard himself being acclaimed the winner. The winner? But what had happened to Drew? Had he had an accident?

All the racers had crossed the finish line, and Jim was holding his new skates and smiling happily when Drew finally dragged in. His face was red and he was frowning.

"What happened, Drew?" Jim cried hurrying up to him.

"What didn't happen?" Drew growled. "Holes have been cut in the ice on the shortcut. I tried to skate around where they had been cut. When I couldn't, I had to skate over the new ice. It was so thin it cracked, and I nearly went under. B-r-r."

"Oh, that's too bad, Drew," the starter said. "We never use the short way for the race because it's such a good spot for ice fishing. I'm sorry. We should have told you."

Drew wrinkled his face. "Smart guys who try to skate on thin ice have nobody to blame but themselves if they fall in."

# First Coal, Then Fire

By Susan Campbell Bartoletti

The basketball banked against the backboard, then dropped through the hoop and bounced on the concrete driveway.

Angie dashed toward the ball, snatching it from an imaginary opponent. She pivoted, faked to the left, then dribbled to the right.

Angie smiled. That last shot made five perfect hook shots in a row—not bad for someone who spends most of each game warming the bench, she thought.

Sure, the hook shot was old-fashioned. But Angie loved the power of the drive, the jump, and the feel of her arm arching over her head. She wished Coach McAllister would let her use it.

Angie's coach wanted her to concentrate on ball handling and leave the shooting to the more experienced players. "Be patient," Coach had said. "The season has just started."

Angie went inside. Nono sat with the checkerboard in the living room. "Who goes first?" Angie asked her grandfather.

"First coal, then fire, my little *pinozza*," said Nono. Angie smiled and slid her coal-black checker forward. Nono called her his "little peanut" because she was tiny. Her basketball teammates stood like trees around her on the court.

"So how is the basketball coming?" asked Nono.

"Good," said Angie, watching her grandfather's move. "If Coach lets me play Thursday, I think I might surprise her." Angie quickly took her turn.

"I watched you from the window," said Nono, rubbing his chin. "You looked very good. Like a dancer." Angie agreed; the hook shot reminded her of a ballerina's leap.

Nono double-jumped two of Angie's pieces.

Surprised, Angie grunted. She thrust a black checker forward and jumped a red. She drummed her fingers on the table, waiting for Nono to make the next move. He seemed to take forever.

Nono fingered one piece, then changed his mind and thought some more. He moved a different one.

"I'm tired of being a bench warmer," said Angie, drawing her knees up to her chest. "But Coach says I have a lot to learn." Angie chewed her lower lip and moved her black checker one square closer to the last row.

Nono grinned slyly. He jumped two of Angie's checkers and landed on the final row. "King me," he said.

Angie groaned. "Never even saw it coming."

Nono tapped Angie's hand. "First coal, then fire, my little *pinozza*," he said. "You must concentrate and have patience."

"Funny," said Angie. "That's just what Coach says about basketball."

Thursday night came. Angie looked around the gym. Nono was sitting where he always sat, seven bleachers behind the Chargers. And Angie was sitting where she always sat, on the bench.

The crowd cheered as each of the starters' names echoed over the loudspeaker. The whistle shrilled. The centers jumped, and the game was under way.

Angie watched anxiously from the bench. The Chargers pressed hard, but the Eagles were good. They hustled and picked their shots carefully. At halftime the Chargers trailed, 22 to 12.

In the locker room Coach McAllister pleaded with the players, "Play defense, girls. Hustle more. You have to *make* winning happen."

Late in the third quarter the Chargers had a scoring streak. They whittled away at the Eagles' lead. When the buzzer sounded, the Chargers were behind by only two points, 28 to 26.

The lead seesawed between the two teams throughout the fourth quarter. Then disaster struck. The Chargers' top scorer fouled out. Angie watched as Coach sent in a substitute. Nervously, Angie glanced at the clock—only fifty-nine seconds were left. The Chargers were down, 36 to 34.

The Chargers' point guard stole the ball, then tripped, sending the ball out-of-bounds. A shudder rippled through the crowd. The guard lay sprawled on the floor, clutching her ankle.

The referee shrilled the whistle. Coach McAllister ran out. The guard hobbled off the floor, leaning on Coach.

"You're in," she said to Angie. "Now, remember, no fancy shots. Think of the team first, and work for the pass underneath."

Angie's heart leaped. Fifty-three seconds left. The Eagles brought the ball into play. Angie stuck to the guard, but the player pivoted and dribbled past her.

Angie's sneakers squeaked against the floor. Coming from behind the guard, Angie snatched the ball away in mid-dribble. She quickly turned and passed to a teammate.

Easy lay-up. The score was tied. Angie's ears rang with the thunder from the stands as her team stole the inbounds pass. Seconds ticked down. Twenty-one. Twenty. The Chargers stalled, passing the ball around as they tried to set up a final, winning shot.

Twelve seconds. Eleven. The gym exploded with excitement. Suddenly, an Eagles player broke away. She stole the ball, then fumbled. Both teams scrambled, but Angie got to the ball first.

The final seconds seemed like slow motion. Angie pivoted and dribbled, driving hard. The crowd went wild, calling Angie's name.

"This is it!" Angie screamed to herself. She jumped. Her arm arched over her head, and the ball shot out toward the basket. It banked off the backboard and plummeted through the hoop. The crowd groaned as the buzzer sounded.

Angie glanced at the flashing scoreboard. She

gasped. The Eagles had won, 38 to 36. She had gone to the wrong basket.

Angie looked over at Coach McAllister. Shaking her head, Coach smiled sadly. Angie's teammates stood speechless.

Slowly, the gym cleared. The team shuffled through the doors to the locker room. Nono walked up and put his arm around Angie's shoulder. "Too much fire?" Angie whispered.

"No, my little *pinozza,*" said Nono. "Not enough coal."

# *Partners*

## By Ellen Javernick

"I'd win for sure if they didn't make us have partners," said Matt.

"Yeah, I know," agreed his friend Brian. "You blazed up Storm Mountain and turned in a great time on the obstacle course. Everyone says you're the best athlete on the whole camping trip."

The camping trip, officially called an Outdoor Education Experience, was a required class for all of the seventh graders at Matt and Brian's school. As the boys walked back from the obstacle course, Brian said, "I bet they make us have partners so we'll get to know guys from other schools. At least your partner seems pretty cool."

"Todd's OK, but he sure can't do many sports," said Matt. "Did you see him put the fifty-pound weight down twice on the obstacle course? That cost him ten seconds each time. We were in second place after this morning's race up the mountain, but I don't even want to *hear* Mr. Caldwell tell us what the standings are this afternoon."

Mr. Caldwell didn't announce the results until everyone had finished cooking supper. The cooking took awhile, because nobody had done much of it before.

At last Mr. Caldwell stood up. "Before I tell you the team scores, I have a new school record to announce. Matt Hewsen's time on the obstacle course was the best anyone has ever had." All the boys cheered, but even though Matt had set a record, he and Todd dropped to third place in team scores.

"Sorry I was so slow," said Todd later as the boys crawled into their sleeping bags. "I'll try harder tomorrow, and maybe we can still win."

"Maybe," said Matt, but he wished he could have competed on his own. The boys were so tired that they fell asleep in spite of the ghost stories they'd heard around the campfire. They slept until Mr. Caldwell banged a spoon on a pan, announcing that it was time to "rise and shine."

After breakfast all the campers met for a short hike to the Cave of the Seven Bears. On the hike Todd and Brian talked about how fast they'd find their way through the cave. Matt wasn't so sure.

"I don't like caves very much," Matt told his friends. "What if we get lost?" The thought scared him a little.

"Don't worry," said Brian. "I hear the cave isn't that tough."

"We'll do fine," said Todd confidently, leaping over a tree limb that had fallen across the trail.

"OK, kids," Mr. Caldwell said when everyone reached the cave's entrance. "For this contest we want both partners to go together. It's not completely dark in there, but you'll save time if you follow the path we've made for you with fluorescent tape. At the end of the cave you slide down through a short tunnel, and I'll record your time when the second partner comes out. Good luck, and may the best team win."

Matt and Todd were the last to go through the cave. Mr. Caldwell punched the button on his stopwatch, and Matt crawled through the opening. Todd was close behind.

The cave was almost totally dark, and it was a minute or two before the boys could see. Slowly, they crawled forward.

"Get away from the opening, Todd," said Matt in a strained voice. He had stopped moving.

Todd looked at Matt in the semi-darkness. "Are you OK?"

Matt's voice trembled. "I *hate* it in here. I'm really scared! I feel like I did once when my brother locked me in the closet. I don't think I can finish. I'm going to crawl back to the entrance." Matt started to turn around in the passageway.

"You can't do that," said Todd. "We'll be disqualified. Grab my arm. Don't talk, and I'll lead you through." Todd squeezed past his partner. The hand that grabbed his was cold but sweaty.

"Everybody is afraid sometimes," Todd said reassuringly. "You're feeling a little claustrophobia. That means fear of closed-in places. I know because I read about a pro football player who gets the same feeling."

Todd pulled Matt forward slowly. "The secret is to stay calm and keep moving. You can see better already, can't you?"

Matt nodded, afraid he'd cry or scream if he said anything. He held on to Todd's arm tightly.

"We're about halfway through," said Todd.

Matt felt a new surge of panic. Now he didn't even know which way he'd run if he completely lost control!

"You're doing just great," Todd said as they rounded a corner and the light became dimmer. Todd led Matt across the narrow space to a spot where the tape appeared to stop. "This is the exit tunnel. Now, all we have got to do is slide down through it."

"No way," said Matt. "It's too dark and too narrow. I'm going back."

"It only lasts a minute," said Todd. "Then you'll be out in the light. You go first, so you won't be stuck inside by yourself."

Todd's calm words made sense. Matt didn't want to be in the cave alone, and the entrance was much too far behind them. Matt closed his eyes, touched the cavern wall with one hand, and took two steps. When he felt the ground slant beneath his feet, he sat down and felt himself sliding forward. By the time Matt opened his eyes, he was in the sunshine again. He breathed a sigh of relief as Todd landed behind him in the grass.

"All right!" shouted Brian as he socked Matt on the back. "You made it!"

"*We* made it," corrected Matt. "I was scared! I might not have gone through if it wasn't for my partner. Todd practically had to drag me the whole way."

"No problem," said Todd with a grin. "After all, that's what partners are for."

# The Right Decision

By Marilyn Kratz

"Hi, Lori!" Jan called as she ran to the corner where she met her best friend each morning. "Did you hear what happened to Kathy?"

"Nothing bad, I hope," said Lori as they started toward school.

"She hurt her knee while roller-skating yesterday," said Jan. "She'll be all right, but her doctor won't let her play basketball for three weeks."

"Three weeks!" groaned Lori. "By that time the basketball season will be over."

"So will our chance to be conference champs," said Jan. "And we had only two more games left to win."

"We'll have a hard time winning without Kathy," said Lori.

"This will probably ruin your chance of breaking the scoring record Brenda Kamlin set last year," said Jan. "Without Kathy to feed you the ball in our number-three offensive play, you won't have enough chances to score."

"Winning is more important," said Lori. But Jan knew how much her friend wanted to top the school record.

"Maybe Miss Barnes will train another girl to replace Kathy," suggested Jan.

"All of our best players are on the first team already," said Lori.

Glumly, the girls entered the Glendale School building and went to their lockers.

"Look, Lori," Jan whispered. "There's a new girl coming in. I wonder if she plays basketball."

"Come on," said Lori. "Let's say hi."

They introduced themselves to the new girl and offered to show her around.

"Thank you," she said. "My name is Barbara Stevens. The principal said I'm going to be in Miss Barnes's homeroom."

"Good," said Lori. "That's our homeroom, too."

"You'll like Miss Barnes," said Jan. "She's our basketball coach. Do you play basketball?"

"I did at the school I used to go to," said Barbara, "but I think I'll be too busy trying to catch up with the classes here to play."

"I'll help you study," offered Jan.

"We really need someone to play forward on our team," added Lori.

"That *is* my favorite position," said Barbara.

The bell interrupted them, and they hurried to their class.

Jan did everything she could to help Barbara that day. She invited Barbara to her home to study that evening.

"You've been a big help," said Barbara after they had finished their lessons. "Maybe I'll have time for basketball after all."

"Great!" exclaimed Jan. "Why don't you come to practice after school tomorrow?"

The next day, as Lori and Jan walked their new friend to the gym, they explained some of the team plays to her. She listened carefully. By the end of the week, she had learned the plays and proved to be good at making baskets. Miss Barnes chose her to take Kathy's place in the starting line-up for Friday evening's game with Centerville.

Barbara seemed nervous as the game began. She moved in too close to the player she was guarding and drew a foul. But then she calmed down, and the rest of the game went well. Glendale won, 54 to 48.

"We're lucky to have you on our team, Barbara," said Jan after the game, "you're good!"

"Not as good as Lori," said Barbara. "She made the most baskets."

"If Lori makes eleven baskets in our last game, she'll top the team scoring record," said Jan.

All that next week, Jan stayed after team practice to help Lori practice shooting baskets. She wanted her friend to be able to top the school scoring record.

Glendale's last game was with the tough Reever City team. The winner of that game would be the conference champ.

Glendale got the ball from the opening jump and Lori scored before the Reever City team could get their defense working. But from there on, neither team had it easy. At halftime, they were tied, 20 to 20. Lori had made five baskets.

"Six more to go," Jan said encouragingly.

"Just so we win!" said Lori.

The second half went better for Glendale. They went into the last quarter with a two-point lead.

Reever City began to press. They got the ball and scored twice.

Then Barbara drew a two-shot free throw and made both points, tying the score with twenty seconds left to play.

Reever City received the ball and moved rapidly toward the basket. The team's forward tried a long shot and missed. Lori got the rebound.

The crowd was on its feet cheering as the players rushed to Glendale's basket.

The ball was passed to Jan. She glanced at the clock. Eight seconds left! Jan knew Lori needed one more basket to top the scoring record, but Lori was being heavily guarded.

Then Jan saw Barbara moving out to the side and into a perfect spot to make a basket.

Jan hesitated a second. What should she do? There was no time to think. Jan passed the ball to Barbara. Barbara made the basket as the buzzer sounded the end of the game.

The crowd rushed down to surround the victorious Glendale team. Jan made her way to Barbara and Lori.

"Lori, I'm sorry . . . ," Jan began.

"Why?" asked Lori. "We won!"

"But you didn't get to break the scoring record," said Jan.

"I can wait till next year," said Lori. "With our team, we'll break all kinds of records."

"You bet we will!" Jan said, smiling at her friends.

# Catching the Big Pike

## By Caryl Chudwin

Jeff thought the night would never end. He jumped out of bed and stood near the cabin window. The sound of the water slapping against the shoreline filled him with excitement. He was really here. He was really going fishing.

"Calm down, Jeff," his father said as he bolted out of his room.

But it wasn't easy. He and his father had planned this fishing trip together. More than anything else, Jeff wanted to show him he could catch the biggest fish in the lake.

Jeff hurried through his breakfast and ran down to the lake. Captain Sam was waiting near his boat. Sam had fished these waters since he was little. He knew where the big pike swam.

Jeff and his father stepped into the boat. Sam carried a wooden chest, fishing rods, and a large net. Sam told Jeff about the fish.

"The northern pike," he said, "live deep in the lake. Each spring, right after the ice melts, they swim to the shallow water of the bays. But only for a while. As the weather grows warmer, they go back to cooler water."

"How can we catch them?" Jeff asked. "They seem smart."

"We'll cast out our lines to a spot in the water where they just might be hiding," Sam answered.

Jeff could hardly wait.

"Hold on tight," Jeff's father said as the boat turned toward open water.

It had been raining most of the night, and Jeff shivered because it was cold. His father zippered Jeff's jacket and lifted its collar around his face. He felt like a stuffed teddy bear. He wore a sweater under his jacket, two pairs of socks, and heavy waterproof boots.

"Look, Dad," he shouted over the motor's roar, "the cabin is getting smaller and smaller." Soon it was out of sight among the tall trees and shrubs on the shore.

After a while the boat slowed down. Sam cut the motor and stopped near a ledge of rocks. He nodded toward a weed bed.

"Weed beds and sunken logs are good places to cast our lines," he said. He took three fishing rods from the bottom of the boat and fastened lures on the end of each line.

The fishing rods were taller than Jeff. Many yards of nylon line were coiled inside the reels at the handles of the rods. A fish could run far with that much line.

Jeff was so impatient to catch a fish that when Sam handed him a fishing rod, he tossed his line carelessly over the side of the boat.

"Come on, pike, bite," he said. Like magic, the line disappeared. Something heavy suddenly sucked it downward.

"A fish," Jeff shouted.

"Put the tip of the rod up," Sam said urgently. "Set the hook."

But it was too late. Jeff had not been prepared. The weight on his rod was suddenly gone. The fish had broken off the hook.

"My first lake fish, and I lost him," groaned Jeff. A frown puckered his forehead.

"We have all day," his father said reassuringly.

He decided then that fishing was only luck.

Then he heard voices in the distance. Jeff turned around and saw another boat. A boy was holding a fishing rod that was almost bent in half. Water sprayed in all directions as a fish slid head-long into a landing net.

"Quick," said Jeff. "Let's go where they are."

His father shook his head. "We can't take another fisherman's place," he said. "That's not fair."

Jeff huddled low in the boat. He was hungry, and his stomach rumbled louder than the motor. He stuck his nose in the collar of his jacket and thought about other fishing times.

In the pond behind his grandmother's house, Jeff had used worms on hooks to catch lots of fish. Once, in the shallow part of a stream, he had almost caught a fish with his bare hands. Jeff looked at the lake and sighed with disappointment.

The sight of the wooden box in the corner of the boat only teased his stomach. It held lunch-time supplies. Sam said there were potatoes, beans, cookies, fruit, and milk inside. He would fry the fish in a pan over an open wood fire—if they caught any. Eating a picnic lunch on a big flat rock would be a new experience for Jeff. He would have to keep trying.

"Dad, please put a new lure on the end of my fishing line," Jeff said, hiding his disappointment. This time he waited until his Dad helped him flip the rod forward toward the weed bed.

Jeff practiced casting out his line with its shiny red-and-white lure. Most important, he practiced raising the tip of the rod to set the hook. It was a lot different from fishing with worms.

Soon the sun peeked through the clouds. It grew brighter and warmer until the sky turned a vivid blue. The wind blew away the last clouds.

"You're a good sport, Jeff," his father said. It made him feel good.

Suddenly Jeff felt something tug at his line. *Zzzzzz* went Jeff's reel as it began to spin. A big silvery fish unreeled his line and carried it toward a rock. He was filled with excitement at the sight of the great fish, but not too excited to think what he must do.

"Give him plenty of line," his father ordered.

Jeff pumped the fishing rod, reeling in a few feet of line at a time. Little by little he brought the fish closer to the boat and Sam's waiting net.

For a second the pike broke the water's surface. Then just as quickly, it dived deep into the water and fought with all its strength. One sharp move and the line might snap.

Jeff wasn't sure he could land the fish. Each time he brought the pike closer to the boat, he pulled away like a gyrating top. His knuckles were white from holding onto the rod so tightly. It seemed like hours had passed.

Finally, the pike relaxed.

Jeff wanted to yell, "I caught him!" but changed his mind. With his father's help he carefully pulled the fish to the side of the boat.

Jeff shouted. "I caught a monster pike."

Sam scooped the dazzling fish into the landing net and lifted it aboard. Its mouth held rows of sharp teeth. Its head was huge. The fish weighed 14 pounds on Sam's spring scale.

"I can't believe I did it," Jeff told his father.

"You worked hard and were patient. And you caught food for our lunch," said Dad, smiling.

"There's a lot more to catching fish than being lucky!" Jeff said thoughtfully.

His Dad and Sam laughed, and Jeff smiled.

# The Banana Kick

By Lois Harris

"Pass the ball to the wing!" yelled the coach on the Striker's team.

With the score 1 to 1, the City Intermediate Soccer Championship Game had gone into overtime. Sheets of rain blew down across the soggy field as the halfback shot the ball to Julie, who turned and started running fast, dribbling the ball with strong, sure kicks. She held her arms out at her sides and bent her knees slightly as she headed up the field toward the goal.

Out of the corner of her eye, Julie saw a flash of blue. She heard her friend Teri yell, "Fullback right behind you."

Changing her direction, Julie headed for the center of the field. The Bulldogs' alert goalie crouched and waited for her.

Julie heard her teammates yelling, "Go, Julie!"

Julie's foot shot the ball toward the goal net, but suddenly a blue streak came between Julie and the ball. The Bulldogs' fullback stopped the ball with the inside of her right foot, and followed with a smooth, sure, left-footed kick of the ball toward her waiting goalie.

"That fullback!" Julie angrily thought to herself. She looked down at her soaked uniform, started to shiver, and suddenly felt tired. But she couldn't give up, because the Strikers had to win. The Bulldogs had been their rivals for three years. And this was the third year the Strikers and the Bulldogs were meeting for the championship game. The last two times the Bulldogs had won.

The Bulldogs' goalie, taking four quick steps, sent the ball halfway down the muddy field to a waiting teammate. Julie whirled and ran back down the field after the ball. She saw two Strikers almost within reach of the ball, but the ball was being relayed from one Bulldog to another.

Julie heard the Bulldogs' coach yell from the sidelines, "Nice passing, girls!"

Desperately, one of the Strikers, the center, intercepted the rocketing ball and kicked it away from the passing Bulldogs.

"What a steal!" Julie thought to herself. Teri, the center, was known for her interceptions. It was her specialty. Julie admired Teri.

Teri kicked the ball to the Strikers' halfback, who had drifted into an open space. The halfback stopped the ball by lightly placing her foot on top of it. Then she quickly shot the ball right over the heads of the approaching Bulldogs. Julie ran toward the ball, bent her knees, and leaned back as the ball smacked her chest. The ball quickly dropped to the ground, and Julie leaned forward and charged up the field, kicking the ball toward the Bulldogs' goalie.

"I've got another chance!" thought Julie as she dribbled the ball to the left and to the right, dodging the Bulldogs as she did so.

She ran faster than she had ever run before, skimming the ball over the ground. The wind blew her wet hair straight back from her red face. She had to make a goal for her team! Suddenly, Julie knew she was ahead of all the others players. She wasn't tired anymore. Julie felt great as she rushed down the field. The Bulldogs' goalie, hoping to stop the ball, ran out to meet her.

Julie heard her teammates yelling, "Go! Go! All the way!"

Taking her eyes off the ball, Julie picked out a spot just to the right of the goalie. But then, out of nowhere, the Bulldogs' fullback reached between the ball and Julie, and hastily kicked the ball toward the sideline.

The Strikers' coach yelled, "Hang in there!" as Julie chased after the fullback and tried to regain control of the ball.

The Bulldogs' fullback swerved and stopped dribbling. Julie was with her and almost took the ball away, but the fullback quickly started dribbling again in the other direction. Julie stayed with her. The fullback dribbled in a zigzag line and faked a move toward the sideline, but Julie wasn't fooled. The fullback stepped backward, and Julie ran forward—kicking the ball against the fullback's leg and right on over the end line! A linesman signaled to the referee with her yellow flag, pointing toward the corner of the field.

"Corner kick," yelled the Strikers' forward as Julie headed for the corner.

Julie looked over at the anxious Bulldogs' goalie and the tense Bulldogs guarding the goal.

Right in the middle of them stood Teri, her arm raised and a finger pointing to her head. She was hoping to head the ball into the goal net.

Julie took a breath and, with the inside of her left foot, sent the ball curving high over the leaping Bulldogs, over Teri who was jumping high, over the goalie's outstretched hands, and right on under the crossbar! A second later a loud whistle blast from the referee signaled the end of the overtime period.

Teri ran up to Julie and grabbed her arm, yelling, "We won!" Julie was surrounded by her happy, yelling teammates.

"We won!"

"Great banana kick!"

"We're the best—champs of the whole city!"

The Strikers' coach ran across the field to the happy team. She gathered the girls around her and said, "Girls, you all played a fine game today. Everyone helped to win the championship. I'm proud of you. This is the moment we've been waiting for."

Coach smiled, and the Strikers started yelling all over again. They felt good.

A white-haired man in a suit hurried across the field. He was an official from the Soccer Association and carried a large, shiny silver cup.

The Strikers' coach said, "Who should accept the cup?"

All together the girls yelled, "Julie!"

The Strikers' coach placed a hand on Julie's shoulder. "Julie, I'd like you to accept the trophy for the team."

Julie turned and looked at the cup. She smiled as the soccer official placed the cup in her hands. Her teammates crowded around. Hardly hearing the words of praise for her team, Julie looked down at the cup and thought, "City champs. The best in the whole city. The Strikers!"

When the soccer official finished his speech, the Strikers gathered around Julie and the cup and let out a big cheer. Gathering the team around her again, the Strikers' coach led them in a big cheer for the Bulldogs. Julie looked across the field at the quiet Bulldog team. They had been silently standing and watching the cup ceremony. Julie headed across the field. She was still carrying the cup. Her teammates followed. Julie walked up to the Bulldogs' fullback and put out her hand. The fullback was looking at the cup. Then she noticed Julie's hand. Slowly, a smile crept across her face as she grasped Julie's hand.

She said, "That was some kick. Where did you learn to do that?"

Julie just smiled. She felt great. She thought to herself, "That was the first banana kick I've ever even tried!"

# The Forgotten Promise

## By Ruth Adams

Michelle thought the last hour of school would never come to an end. This was the third day of the cold snap, and today the pond would be hard enough for skating. She had made plans with Tina and Barb during lunch hour. They were going straight home from school to get their skates. In just a month the first trials to qualify for the regional figure skating championship would begin. All three girls were sure they would have a chance at winning this year, but practice was crucial.

Michelle stared dreamily out the classroom window. It had been snowing hard most of the day and she guessed that there must be at least eight inches of snow on the ground. They would have to shovel the snow off the pond before they could skate. If they didn't, it would get packed down and become too bumpy for skating. Michelle liked the idea of shoveling snow on ice skates. By pushing the snow ahead and skating behind, she thought she could go as fast as the street plows.

It had stopped snowing when Michelle bounded out of the school building. The snow lay so perfect and white and peaceful that she thought it was a shame to spoil it by walking on it.

However, the boys and girls soon trampled it. Michelle reached down and grabbed a handful of snow and threw it high in the air. Just for fun. Just to feel the cold, wet crystals come drifting down on her upturned face.

Michelle ran all the way home and burst into the house, shouting. "Mom! I'm going skating!"

She had already changed her clothes and was getting her skates out of the closet when her mother came from the kitchen. A small frown puckered her forehead.

"Haven't you forgotten something, Michelle?" she asked.

Michelle turned up a puzzled face. "Forgotten something?" she muttered. "I don't think so."

"It snowed today," hinted her mother.

The puzzlement on Michelle's face turned to dismay as she slapped her hand to her forehead.

"Oh, boy," she groaned. "I promised to shovel the walk for Mrs. Ericson this winter!"

"The front *and* the back walks," reminded Mother in a kind, but firm, tone.

"Can't I do it tomorrow? I have to practice for the figure skating competition." Michelle's voice rose in disappointment.

"I know how important the competition is to you," Mother replied. "But Mrs. Ericson is very old and could be seriously hurt if she fell in the snow."

Mother went back into the kitchen.

"Oh, boy," Michelle groaned again.

She was still sitting in the middle of the hall closet a few minutes later when her friends knocked on the door. She got up slowly and went to let them in.

"You don't look very happy," said Barb. "What's wrong? Why aren't you ready to go? We've got a lot of practicing to do."

"Hurry up and get your skates, Michelle," said Tina impatiently. "The pond will be full of kids before we get there."

"I can't go," said Michelle. "I have to shovel the walks for Mrs. Ericson."

"Oh, do it some other time," said Tina. "The pond is just perfect for skating today, and we *have* to practice."

"No, I promised," said Michelle. "And I do want to help her out. I just wish it weren't today."

"Well, you can go tomorrow, I guess," said Tina regretfully. "But I was hoping you and Barb could help me with my routine."

"I can't go tomorrow," said Barb. "I promised my brother I would do his paper route for him."

The thought of missing two afternoons of practice made the girls feel miserable.

Suddenly, Michelle had an idea.

"I tell you what," she said. "You two help me shovel Mrs. Ericson's walks today. Then, if Tina and I help you with the papers tomorrow, Barb, we can still go skating both afternoons. The work will go faster if we do it together."

"We won't have as much time for skating, though," said Tina.

"We'll just have to practice harder and skate faster," chuckled Michelle as she struggled into her jacket. "Come on. Let's get to work!"